MY BROWN BEAR BARNEY

By Dorothy Butler
Illustrated by Elizabeth Fuller

A TRUMPET CLUB SPECIAL EDITION

Published by The Trumpet Club
666 Fifth Avenue, New York, New York
10103

ISBN 0-440-84768-0

This edition published by arrangement
with Greenwillow Books, a division of
William Morrow & Company, Inc.
Printed in the United States of America
September 1992

1 3 5 7 9 10 8 6 4 2
DAN

When I go shopping, I take . . .

my mother, my little brother, my yellow basket,
my red umbrella

and my brown bear Barney.

When I play with my friend Fred,
I take . . .

my bike, our old dog Charlie, two apples from our tree,
my boots

and my brown bear Barney.

When I go gardening, I take . . .

my father, my straw hat, my wheelbarrow, my spade

and my brown bear Barney.

When I go to the beach, I take . . .

my mother, my father, my little brother, special things to eat,
my sunglasses

and my brown bear Barney.

When I go to my grandmother's,
I take . . .

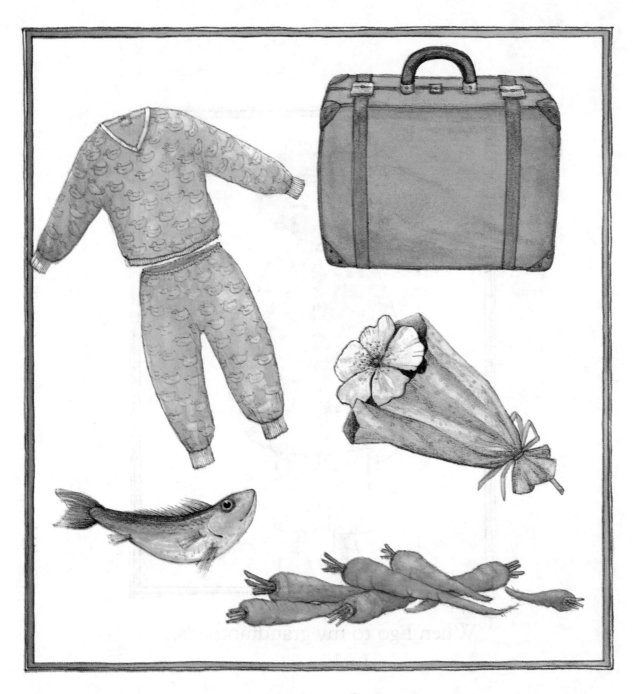

my pajamas in a suitcase, a flower in green paper,
a tasty tidbit for her cat, some carrots from my garden

and my brown bear Barney.

When I go to bed, I take . . .

a good book or two, our old dog Charlie,
an apple for the morning, my big silver flashlight

and my brown bear Barney.

When I go to school, next year or the next,
I'll take . . .

a new school bag, some lunch, my dinosaur badge and
a pencil with an eraser on the end.

But not my brown bear Barney.
My mother says that bears don't go to school.

We'll see about that!